# Thomas Jefferson
## Father of Our Democracy

# Thomas Jefferson

## Father of Our Democracy

A FIRST BIOGRAPHY

BY

David A. Adler

ILLUSTRATED BY

Jacqueline Garrick

*Holiday House/New York*

# IMPORTANT DATES

| | |
|---|---|
| 1743 | Born April 13 in Albemarle County, Virginia. |
| 1760–1762 | Studied at the College of William and Mary. |
| 1762–1767 | Studied law with George Wythe and passed an examination to practice law. |
| 1767–1768 | Designed and began construction of his home, Monticello. |
| 1769–1775 | Served in the Virginia House of Burgesses. |
| 1772 | Married Martha Wayles Skelton. |
| 1776 | Wrote the Declaration of Independence. |
| 1776–1779 | Served in the Virginia House of Delegates. |
| 1779–1781 | Governor of Virginia. |
| 1782 | Martha Jefferson, his wife, died. |
| 1781–1785 | Wrote *Notes on the State of Virginia*. |
| 1785–1789 | Minister to France. |
| 1790–1793 | Secretary of State in President Washington's cabinet. |
| 1797–1801 | Vice President of the United States. |
| 1801–1809 | Third President of the United States. |
| 1825 | The University of Virginia opened. |
| 1826 | Died July 4 at Monticello. |

# CONTENTS

# 1. Shadwell

In 1743, when Thomas Jefferson was born, no one knew that one day he would be president of the United States. No one even knew that one day there would be a United States.

Thomas Jefferson was born in Virginia. It was an English royal colony. George the Second was the king of England and the people of Virginia were loyal to their king.

In 1743, along the coast and some rivers of Virginia, were great tobacco plantations with large houses. Ships with clothes, books, newspapers, and letters from England sailed to the shores of these plantations. But Thomas Jefferson was born further inland. Just beyond his home, to the west, was wild unsettled land—the American frontier.

Thomas was born in a four-room wooden house. His father named the house and the land around it Shadwell after the place in London, England, where Mrs. Jefferson was born.

Squirrels, wild turkeys, and deer ran past the front porch of the house. And in the woods beyond were wolves, panthers, and bears. When Thomas was old enough to use a gun, he went into those woods looking for squirrels and turkeys to shoot. But he was especially looking for wolves. In that part of Virginia, whoever killed a wolf was given a reward of one hundred and forty pounds of tobacco leaves.

Young Thomas had red hair, freckles, and a pointed chin and nose. He would one day grow to be as tall as his father, Peter, but not as strong. People in Virginia spoke often about the strength of Peter Jefferson. They said that once, when three men together couldn't pull down an old shack, Peter tied a rope around the shack and pulled it down himself. And they spoke of the time Peter stood between two casks of tobacco weighing one thousand pounds each. The casks were lying on the ground and with one hand on each, Peter pushed them both up at the same time.

Thomas's mother was Jane Jefferson. She was a warm and friendly woman. She loved to write. One day Thomas would love to write, too.

Jane Jefferson was from one of the leading landowning families of Virginia. Her father, Isham Randolph, was well known throughout the colony. He was a seafaring man and was called Captain by his many friends. He owned a few thousand acres of

choice Virginia land. He was one of the richest men in the
colony.

Isham once paid the boat passage for two men who wanted to
come to the colonies from England. He paid on the condition
that when they arrived in Virginia, they would work for him and
make, among other things, two hundred and fifty pairs of shoes.
That's a lot of shoes. Isham needed them for his slaves.

In 1743, when Thomas was born, there were slaves throughout Virginia. The slaves were black people who were hunted in
Africa, caught, and locked in chains. They were brought thou-
sands of miles by boat to the colonies and then sold. A plantation
owner could buy a slave for about one hundred twenty-five
dollars and own him for life. Slaves cleared the fields, planted,
harvested, and cured the tobacco, cooked and served the meals,
and worked as tailors, shoemakers, coachmen, and carpenters.

Young Thomas was surrounded by slaves. Later, when he
became a member of the Virginia government, and of the government of the new United States, he tried to pass laws ending
the buying and selling of slaves. He called slavery barbarous,
cruel, and shameful. He proposed that young slaves be edu-

cated. When the women became eighteen and the men twenty-one, he wanted them to be given tools, seeds, cows, and guns, and then taken to Africa and set free.

But even with all his plans, Thomas grew up to have slaves of his own—at times more than two hundred. He inherited the slaves from his and his wife's parents. He was known to be a good master, but he was also criticized for not letting his slaves go free.

When Thomas was older, he wouldn't remember his first years at Shadwell. His earliest memory would be of being lifted onto a horse at the age of two and riding with a slave on a three-day, seventy-mile journey from Shadwell to Tuckahoe.

# 2. *Tuckahoe*

Tuckahoe was a large, beautiful house surrounded by flower gardens and tobacco fields. It had belonged to William Randolph, Jane's cousin and Peter Jefferson's good friend. When William Randolph and his wife died, the Jeffersons moved to Tuckahoe to care for the house, the fields, and for the three Randolph children, Judith, Mary and Thomas.

Peter and Jane Jefferson had four children of their own. There was Thomas, who was then two years old, his two older sisters, Jane and Mary, and the baby, Elizabeth. Between the two families, there were seven children at Tuckahoe. It became a busy, happy place.

While the Jeffersons lived at Tuckahoe another girl was born, Martha. Two boys were born there, too, but they died soon after birth. Later, after the Jeffersons moved back to Shadwell, there would be three more children: Lucy and the twins, Anna Scott and Randolph. Thomas was the third oldest of the eight Jefferson children.

Behind the house at Tuckahoe were apple and peach trees. And there were many smaller buildings. There was a one-room building where fat was boiled and made into soap. There were smokehouses where meat was cured. There were houses where tobacco leaves were dried. There were barns, stables, and beyond them, houses for the slaves. And there was a small one-room wooden schoolhouse.

When Thomas was five he had his first lessons in that schoolhouse. Peter Jefferson hired a private teacher who taught the children arithmetic, reading, and especially penmanship. An easy-to-read handwriting was considered a sign of a good education. Thomas spent many hours dipping his goose-quill pen into a small ink bottle and practicing his script. But he didn't always write on paper, as he should have. He once wrote his name on the wall of the schoolhouse.

When Thomas Jefferson was nine, his family returned to Shadwell. But Thomas didn't spend much time there. His father felt that Thomas needed to learn Latin and Greek, so he could read the classics by Virgil, Cato, and Homer. He sent his son to Dover Creek, near Tuckahoe. Thomas lived and studied at Dover Creek for more than five years with Reverend William Douglas.

Thomas didn't consider Reverend Douglas to be a very good teacher of Latin or Greek. How could he be? According to Thomas, Reverend Douglas didn't know much of either language himself.

In 1757 Thomas's father died. Peter Jefferson was just forty-nine years old. He left a considerable estate—a few thousand acres of land, more than sixty slaves, and a great many horses, cattle, and hogs. Among the items willed to Thomas were his father's forty books, including a Bible, a prayer book, a book of English history, and the works of William Shakespeare. This was the beginning of Thomas's lifelong love of books.

Many years later, the small Library of Congress was burned by the British during the War of 1812. Thomas Jefferson sold his books to the United States Congress in 1815. His collection became the beginning of what would become one of the largest libraries in the world.

Thomas's education did not end after his father's death. He studied for two years with Reverend James Maury, a man Thomas greatly respected. Reverend Maury lived with his large family in a log cabin just fourteen miles from Shadwell.

While Thomas was living and studying with Reverend Maury, he met Dabney Carr. Dabney rode a swift horse, much faster than the one Thomas rode. Thomas bet that Dabney couldn't beat him in a horse race on February 30. Days passed, and at the

end of February Dabney realized that he had been tricked. Of course he couldn't beat Thomas in a race on February 30. February didn't have thirty days.

Thomas won the bet and he won a friend. Many years later Thomas would say that of all the men he met and knew, he liked Dabney the best.

Thomas could have decided to end his education after he left Reverend Maury. He had enough land to support himself by growing and selling tobacco. But Thomas loved to learn. He would go to college.

# 3. *Williamsburg*

In the spring of 1760, sixteen-year-old Thomas Jefferson went to the College of William and Mary in Williamsburg, the capital of colonial Virginia. There were just three hundred houses in Williamsburg, and fewer than two thousand people lived there. But it was the largest city Thomas had ever seen.

Virginia was governed by the royal governor who represented the king of England and by burgesses who represented the people of Virginia. Whenever the House of Burgesses was at work, a few thousand additional people came to Williamsburg, crowding the inns and streets. Peter Jefferson and Isham Randolph had served as burgesses. In 1760, when Thomas first came to Williamsburg, George Washington was a burgess.

Thomas was a good singer and dancer and an expert at playing the violin. He was often invited to the governor's palace to play with Governor Francis Fauquier and with George Wythe, a great lawyer and a member of the House of Burgesses.

During his first year at college, Thomas spent time at horse races, card games, and fox hunts. But after that, he became a more serious student, studying fifteen hours a day, from early morning until very late at night. It is perhaps during his years at college that he first said, ''It is wonderful how much may be done, if we are always doing.'' And Thomas was always doing.

Thomas wanted to be a lawyer. After college Thomas worked in the law office of his friend George Wythe. He helped George Wythe prepare his cases. He watched him in court. He read his law books. After five years of work and study, Thomas took an examination, passed it, and was allowed to practice law.

# 4.  *The Coming Revolution*

It would be quite some years before the American Revolution. But the problems which caused it were already beginning.

In the early 1760s England fought a war with France and won huge areas of land in the New World. But fighting the war cost money, and keeping soldiers in the colonies and the land beyond them which England had just won would cost more money. King George the Third of England decided to tax the colonies. In 1765 the Stamp Act was passed. Newspapers, contracts, and other papers the colonists used had to have a stamp on them sold by the government.

Thomas Jefferson went to the House of Burgesses to hear another young lawyer, his friend Patrick Henry, speak out against the Stamp Act. Patrick Henry protested paying English taxes without having a voice in English government. He was a strong speaker and relied on the power of his voice and his words to win his point. But Patrick Henry's speech against the king was too strong for many of those listening. It was interrupted by cries of ''Treason!'' But it wasn't too strong for Thomas Jefferson. He agreed with Patrick Henry.

Unlike his friend, Thomas Jefferson was a poor speaker with a weak voice. If he spoke too long or too loud, he became hoarse. As a lawyer, Thomas had many clients and he spent many hours preparing their cases. He relied on hard work and the power of his ideas.

During the first seven years after Thomas became a lawyer, he had hundreds of cases, but many were with clients too poor to pay for his work. During those years, he began to build a house of his own, which he designed, on a small mountain near Shadwell. He called the house Monticello which is Italian for Little Mountain. And in 1768 he was elected to the House of Burgesses.

*Monticello in 1809*

A few days after Thomas joined the House of Burgesses, the royal governor dismissed all its members. He didn't like some of the resolutions they passed, especially that the thirteen colonies resolved to work together to voice their complaints against England.

There was a new election to the House of Burgesses. Thomas Jefferson and the eighty-four other burgesses who stood firm against England were elected again. The twenty-three burgesses who were not willing to protest the new taxes were not re-elected.

Soon after Thomas was elected and re-elected to the House of Burgesses, he began visiting the home of John Wayles, a lawyer. But it wasn't John Wayles who Thomas went to see. It was his daughter, Martha Wayles Skelton. She was a widow. Her husband had died after only two years of marriage. She was a smart, pretty woman with reddish-brown hair and hazel eyes. And she loved music.

Other men were interested, too, in marrying Martha. According to one story, two men came on one night. Each planned to ask Martha to marry him. But as they came closer to the house, they heard music—the sounds of Martha playing the harpsichord and Thomas playing the violin. Then they heard Martha and Thomas singing together. And the two men left, without ever telling Martha why they had come.

Thomas Jefferson and Martha Wayles Skelton were married on New Year's Day, 1772.

# 5. *The Declaration of Independence*

During the next few years, after his marriage to Martha Wayles Skelton, Thomas Jefferson was at the center of Virginia's protests against the English.

Early in 1775, in a church in Richmond, Virginia, Patrick Henry cried out, "Give me liberty or give me death!" His words were repeated by patriots throughout the colonies. And on April 19, 1775, farmers in Lexington and Concord, Massachusetts, fired their guns at English soldiers. The Revolutionary War had begun. It lasted eight years, until 1783, when the colonies won their freedom from England.

Soon after the war began, Thomas Jefferson was in Philadelphia, at a meeting of the Continental Congress. He was meeting with delegates from other colonies. They needed a written declaration of their independence. Thomas Jefferson wrote it. A few changes were made by members of the congress and on July 4, 1776, the Declaration of Independence was approved.

The words of Thomas Jefferson, which were later signed by fifty-six members of the Continental Congress, are among the most famous and most important words ever written.

He wrote, "We hold these truths to be self-evident, that all men are created equal, that they are endowed by their Creator with certain unalienable Rights, that among these are Life, Liberty and the pursuit of Happiness."

In the Declaration of Independence, Thomas Jefferson wrote that all people have the right to be free. Governments are meant to serve the people. He listed the many unfair acts of King George the Third. He wrote that the Continental Congress appealed to the king, then to the people of England, but when fair treatment was refused, the colonists had no choice but to declare their independence.

In September 1776, just after the Declaration of Independence was approved, Thomas Jefferson returned to Virginia. There was no longer a royal governor sent from England. Patrick Henry was the governor of Virginia. And there was no longer a House of Burgesses. There was a House of Delegates. Thomas Jefferson was one of the delegates.

This was a time of change. Thomas helped to rewrite many of the laws of Virginia, to make them more just. He helped bring religious freedom to Virginia.

Not all of Thomas Jefferson's ideas immediately became law. He urged that children be offered free education, paid for by the state. He felt that only an educated people could remain free. The lawmakers in Virginia were not ready for this.

Thomas Jefferson was elected governor in 1779 and 1780. And while he was governor, English soldiers attacked Virginia. Soldiers even came after Jefferson. He was warned and left the house with just minutes to spare.

In 1781, after his term as governor ended, Thomas Jefferson wrote a book called *Notes on Virginia*. In it he described Virginia, its history, its rivers, trees, and minerals, and its people. He also wrote his thoughts on many things. He wrote that most wars were a foolish waste of money and lives to gain a little land. Slavery was evil. The Indians were being unfairly treated. And he wrote strong words about the right of every man to have freedom of religion—to serve, as he wrote, ''twenty gods or no god.''

In 1782 Thomas Jefferson's wife Martha became ill. Thomas stayed near her, nursing her for four months. But in September she died. She was a young woman, just thirty-three.

Thomas could not be comforted. Just before she died, he fainted and fell to the floor. For three weeks after she died, he would not leave his room. Then for hours each day, he rode on his horse wildly through the fields and woods near his house.

Thomas and Martha had six children, but only two, Martha (''Patsy'') and Mary (''Polly'') lived beyond their third birthdays. Thomas never married again.

# 6. *Off to France*

Thomas felt a real emptiness after his wife died. He was pleased in 1783 when he was elected to Congress. As a member of Congress, Thomas helped design our money system. We have pennies, dimes, and dollars because Thomas Jefferson and Gouverneur Morris of New York felt it would be easiest to base our money on the number ten. Thomas also helped pass the treaty which ended the Revolutionary War.

The next year, 1784, Thomas was sent to France. Benjamin Franklin and John Adams were already there. Together they worked out trade agreements with the countries of Europe.

Thomas spent five happy years in France. He enjoyed the Old World music, art, and architecture. He bought books, met interesting people, and tasted the delicious French foods and wines.

While Thomas Jefferson was in France, the American government was being reorganized, and a constitution was being written. Jefferson's friend James Madison sent it to France for Thomas to read. He liked it, but felt something was missing—a bill of rights. A short time later, with the leadership of James Madison, the first ten amendments, the Bill of Rights, were added to the Constitution. Among the many freedoms they guarantee are the freedoms of speech, the press, and religion.

In 1789 Thomas Jefferson returned home to Virginia. But soon he traveled to New York City. It was then the capital of the new United States and President George Washington had asked Thomas to join the government as Secretary of State. He would be responsible for the new country's dealings with other nations and with the American Indians. He would also be responsible for lighthouses, the minting of coins, new inventions, and weights and measures.

Thomas had real differences with another member of the government, the Secretary of the Treasury, Alexander Hamilton of New York. Jefferson believed the government belonged to all the people. Hamilton wanted the rich to control the government. The differences between the two led to the first political parties. Jefferson's followers became the Democrat-Republicans. Hamilton's became the Federalists.

In 1796, the first two-party election for president was held. John Adams, the Federalist, narrowly beat Thomas Jefferson, the Democrat-Republican. According to the law then, Thomas Jefferson became vice president since he had the second highest number of votes.

Four years later, in 1800, Thomas Jefferson was elected the third president of the United States. He was a very popular president and was re-elected in 1804.

# 7. *President Thomas Jefferson*

Thomas Jefferson was the first president to be inaugurated in the new capital, Washington D.C. It was not a city then, but a muddy wilderness with some buildings, many of them only half finished. Even the White House wasn't completely built. It didn't have its famous white columns.

People liked to call the White House the president's palace. But Thomas Jefferson didn't look like he belonged in a palace. Some Federalists complained that he dressed in old clothes and woolen socks, that there were no buckles on his shoes, and that the heels were not high enough. But Thomas Jefferson felt the president represented the people of his country and should dress like them, too.

By the windows of his study in the White House, Thomas grew flowers. And in one of the windows, above the flowers, hung a cage with a mockingbird inside. When Thomas was alone, he let the bird fly out of the cage. It often perched on the President's shoulder. It even ate food from the President's lips.

Thomas Jefferson insisted that people not bow to him. He shook their hands instead. And he didn't want the country to celebrate his birthday, so he didn't tell anyone when it was.

In 1801, soon after Thomas Jefferson became president, he declared war on Tripoli, a North African state of pirates. The United States had been paying a ransom to keep the pirates of Tripoli from attacking American ships. Thomas Jefferson refused to pay. He sent ships instead to fight the pirates. And after four years of fighting, the pirates dropped their demand for payment.

In 1803 Thomas Jefferson purchased for the United States a huge area of land from France. The land stretched from the Mississippi River to the Rocky Mountains. It was called the Louisiana Purchase. It doubled the size of the United States.

The land purchased from France was an unknown wilderness. In 1804, at the urging of Thomas Jefferson, Congress paid Meriwether Lewis and William Clark along with about forty young men to explore the land west of the Mississippi River. They explored all the way to the Pacific Ocean, began peaceful relations with some Indian tribes, and helped open the West to settlers.

While Thomas Jefferson was president, he lowered taxes and the number of people who worked for the government. He tried to keep the government out of people's lives.

In 1809, when his second term as president ended, Thomas Jefferson returned to Virginia, to the home he called Monticello.

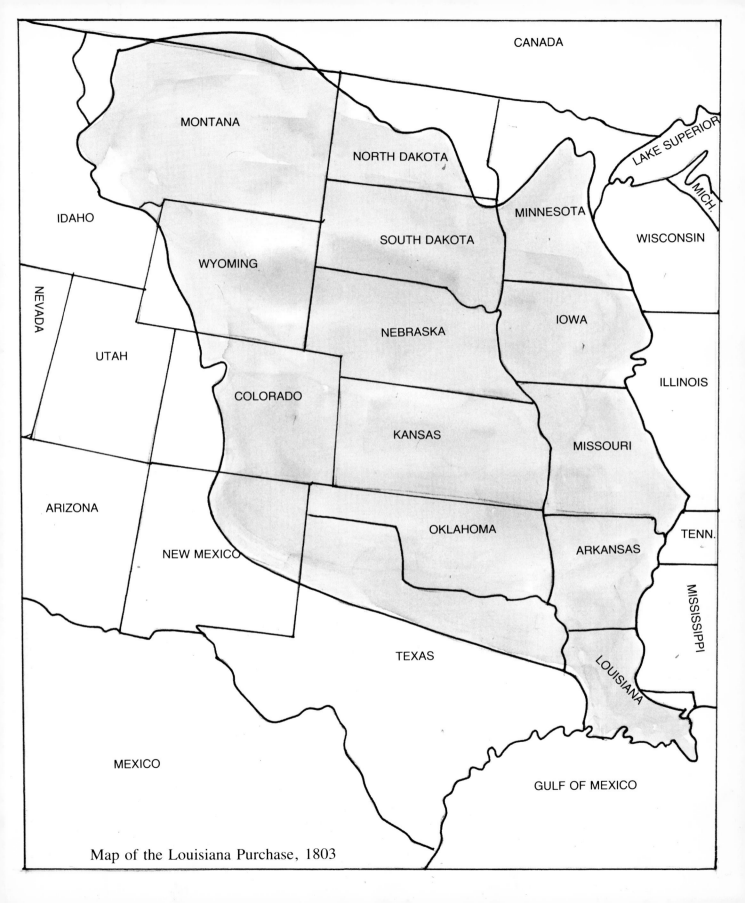

CANADA

MONTANA

NORTH DAKOTA

LAKE SUPERIOR

MICH.

IDAHO

MINNESOTA

WISCONSIN

SOUTH DAKOTA

WYOMING

NEVADA

IOWA

NEBRASKA

UTAH

ILLINOIS

COLORADO

KANSAS

MISSOURI

ARIZONA

OKLAHOMA

TENN.

NEW MEXICO

ARKANSAS

MISSISSIPPI

TEXAS

LOUISIANA

MEXICO

GULF OF MEXICO

Map of the Louisiana Purchase, 1803

*moldboard plow*

# 8. *The Sage of Monticello*

In the last years of his life Thomas Jefferson was called the Sage of Monticello, and many people, including presidents of the United States, wrote to him and visited him to ask for advice.

Now Thomas had time for his many interests—architecture, gardening, books, music, and his inventions. Among his many inventions was an improved moldboard for a plow. It made it easier to pull the plow through the soil. He was awarded a gold medal for this invention by the Agricultural Society of Paris.

He designed a table with a top that could be raised and lowered. He could use that table when he was sitting or standing.

He also designed a dumbwaiter, a box which was moved with ropes between the dining room and the wine cellar below.

During the years after he was president, Thomas Jefferson helped establish the University of Virginia. He chose the subjects to be taught and the professors to teach them. He designed the buildings, hired the workers, and supervised them as they built the university.

*architect's table*

*wine dumbwaiter in side of chimneypiece*

Thomas received well over one thousand letters a year. Some of the letters were from John Adams, the second president of the United States.

Jefferson and Adams wrote to each other about many things including religion, politics, and their grandchildren. Through their letters they became, once again, close, dear friends. And on July 4, 1826, exactly fifty years after the Declaration of Independence was signed by them, both men died.

Thomas Jefferson had lived a full eighty-three years. He did so much so well. He was one of America's most talented men.

Thomas Jefferson had been a farmer, lawyer, architect, inventor, musician, burgess, ambassador, governor, secretary of state, vice president, and president.

Thomas Jefferson is considered one of our greatest leaders. Because he believed people should govern themselves and because many of his ideas helped to shape our government, he has been called The Father of Democracy.

Among Thomas Jefferson's papers his family found a drawing of the type of tombstone he wanted. And he wrote the few words he wanted written on it, how he wanted to be remembered:

*Here was buried*
*Thomas Jefferson*
*Author of the Declaration of American Independence*
*of the Statute of Virginia for Religious Freedom*
*and Father of the University of Virginia.*

# INDEX

For DIANE MASON, a good friend
and a great librarian

Text copyright © 1987 by David A. Adler
Illustrations copyright © 1987 by Jacqueline Garrick
All rights reserved
Printed in the United States of America
First Edition

Library of Congress Cataloging-in-Publication Data

Adler, David A.
Thomas Jefferson, father of our democracy.

Includes index.
SUMMARY: An account of Jefferson's life highlighting his many accomplishments as governor, architect, gardener, inventor, and President.
1. Jefferson, Thomas, 1743–1826—Juvenile literature. 2. Presidents—United States—Biography—Juvenile literature. [1. Jefferson, Thomas, 1743-1826. 2. Presidents] I. Garrick, Jacqueline, ill. II. Title
E332.79.A26   1987      973.4'6'0924     [B]  [92]      87-45336
ISBN 0-8234-0667-9